Editor's Note

What are nonsense verses? Poetry that doesn't make a bit of sense, of course. Nonsense poetry begins with Mother Goose rhymes. What could be more nonsensical than a cow jumping over the moon? Or an elephant jumping so high he touches the sky? But that certainly isn't where nonsense poetry stops.

Such masters of nonsense verse as Lewis Carroll and Edward Lear carried nonsense to a high rarely equaled in modern times. And what good is nonsense, you may ask. Rhyme, rhythm, words—wonderful, absurd words—and most of all, laughter, would be the answer!

JABBERWOCKY
and Other
Nonsense Verses

Edited by H. E. Casterline
Illustrated by Jean Chandler

A GOLDEN BOOK • NEW YORK
Western Publishing Company, Inc., Racine, Wisconsin 53404

Jabberwocky

'Twas brillig, and the slithy toves
    Did gyre and gimble in the wabe;
All mimsy were the borogoves,
    And the mome raths outgrabe.

"Beware the Jabberwock, my son!
    The jaws that bite, the claws that catch!
Beware the Jubjub bird, and shun
    The frumious Bandersnatch!"

He took his vorpal sword in hand;
    Long time the manxome foe he sought—
So rested he by the Tumtum tree,
    And stood awhile in thought.

And as in uffish thought he stood,
    The Jabberwock, with eyes of flame,
Came whiffling through the tulgey wood,
    And burbled as it came!

One, two! One, two! And through and through
    The vorpal blade went snicker-snack!
He left it dead, and with its head
    He went galumphing back.

"And hast thou slain the Jabberwock?
    Come to my arms, my beamish boy!
O frabjous day! Callooh! Callay!"
    He chortled in his joy.

'Twas brillig, and the slithy toves
    Did gyre and gimble in the wabe;
All mimsy were the borogoves,
    And the mome raths outgrabe.

—*Lewis Carroll*

As I was going out one day,
My head fell off and rolled away.
But when I saw that it was gone,
I picked it up and put it on.

And when I got into the street,
A fellow cried: "Look at your feet!"
I looked at them and sadly said:
"I've left them both asleep in bed!"

—*Anonymous*

The Twins

In form and feature, face and limb,
I grew so like my brother,
That folks got taking me for him,
And each for one another.
It puzzled all our kith and kin,
It reached an awful pitch;
For one of us was born a twin,
Yet not a soul knew which.

One day (to make the matter worse),
Before our names were fixed,
As we were being washed by nurse
We got completely mixed;
And thus, you see, by Fate's decree,
(Or rather nurse's whim),
My brother John got christened *me*,
And I got christened *him*.

This fatal likeness even dogged
    My footsteps when at school,
And I was always getting flogged,
    For John turned out a fool.
I put this question hopelessly
    To everyone I knew—
What *would* you do, if you were me,
    To prove that you were *you*?

Our close resemblance turned the tide
    Of my domestic life;
For somehow my intended bride
    Became my brother's wife.
In short, year after year the same
    Absurd mistakes went on;
And when I died—the neighbors came
    And buried brother John!

        —*Henry S. Leigh*

The Little Man

As I was walking up the stair
I met a man who wasn't there.
He wasn't there again today.
I wish, I wish, he'd stay away.

—*Hughes Mearns*

The Owl and the Pussy-Cat

The Owl and the Pussy-Cat went to sea
    In a beautiful pea-green boat:
They took some honey, and plenty of money
    Wrapped up in a five-pound note.
The Owl looked up to the stars above,
    And sang to a small guitar,
"O lovely Pussy, O Pussy, my love,
    What a beautiful Pussy you are,
        You are,
        You are,
What a beautiful Pussy you are!"

Pussy said to the Owl, "You elegant fowl,
  How charmingly sweet you sing!
Oh! let us be married; too long we have tarried:
  But what shall we do for a ring?"
They sailed away, for a year and a day,
  To the land where the bong-tree grows;
And there in a wood a Piggy-wig stood,
  With a ring at the end of his nose,
    His nose,
    His nose,
  With a ring at the end of his nose.

"Dear Pig, are you willing to sell for one shilling
    Your ring?" Said the Piggy, "I will."
So they took it away, and were married next day
    By the turkey who lives on the hill.
They dined on mince and slices of quince,
    Which they ate with a runcible spoon;
And hand in hand, on the edge of the sand,
    They danced by the light of the moon,
        The moon,
        The moon,
They danced by the light of the moon.

              —Edward Lear

There once was an old man of Brest,
Who always was funnily drest:
    He wore gloves on his nose,
    And a hat on his toes,
And a boot in the midst of his chest.

—Cosmo Monkhouse

An epicure, dining at Crewe,
Found quite a large mouse in his stew.
    Said the waiter, "Don't shout,
    And wave it about,
Or the rest will be wanting one, too!"

—Anonymous

Father William

"You are old, Father William," the young man said,
    "And your hair has become very white;
And yet you incessantly stand on your head—
    Do you think, at your age, it is right?"

"In my youth," Father William replied to his son,
    "I feared it might injure the brain;
But now that I'm perfectly sure I have none,
    Why, I do it again and again."

"You are old," said the youth, "as I mentioned before,
    And have grown most uncommonly fat;
Yet you turned a back somersault in at the door—
    Pray, what is the reason of that?"

"In my youth," said the sage, as he shook his gray locks,
    "I kept all my limbs very supple
By the use of this ointment—one shilling the box—
    Allow me to sell you a couple."

"You are old," said the youth, "and your jaws are too weak
    For anything tougher than suet;
Yet you finished the goose, with the bones and the beak—
    Pray, how did you manage to do it?"

"In my youth," said his father, "I took to the law,
    And argued each case with my wife;
And the muscular strength, which it gave to my jaw,
    Has lasted the rest of my life."

"You are old," said the youth, "one would hardly suppose
    That your eye was as steady as ever;
Yet you balanced an eel on the end of your nose—
    What made you so awfully clever?"

"I have answered three questions, and that is enough,"
    Said his father, "don't give yourself airs!
Do you think I can listen all day to such stuff?
    Be off, or I'll kick you downstairs!"

—*Lewis Carroll*

'Twas midnight on the ocean,
Not a streetcar was in sight;
The sun was shining brightly,
For it rained all day that night.
'Twas a summer day in winter
And snow was raining fast,
As a barefoot boy with shoes on
Stood sitting in the grass.

—*Anonymous*

The Walloping Window-Blind

A capital ship for an ocean trip
    Was The Walloping Window-Blind;
No gale that blew dismayed her crew
    Or troubled the captain's mind.
The man at the wheel was taught to feel
    Contempt for the wildest blow,
And it often appeared, when the weather had cleared,
    That he'd been in his bunk below.

The boatswain's mate was very sedate,
    Yet fond of amusement, too;
And he played hopscotch with the starboard watch
    While the captain tickled the crew.
And the gunner we had was apparently mad,
    For he sat on the after-rail,
And fired salutes with the captain's boots,
    In the teeth of the booming gale.

The captain sat in a commodore's hat,
    And dined, in a royal way,
On toasted pigs and pickles and figs
    And gummery bread, each day.
But the cook was Dutch, and behaved as such;
    For the food that he gave the crew
Was a number of tons of hot-cross buns,
    Chopped up with sugar and glue.

And we all felt ill as mariners will,
    On a diet that's cheap and rude;
And we shivered and shook as we dipped the cook
    In a tub of his gluesome food.
Then nautical pride we laid aside,
    And we cast the vessel ashore
On the Gulliby Isles, where the Poohpooh smiles,
    And the Anagazanders roar.

Composed of sand was that favored land,
    And trimmed with cinnamon straws;
And pink and blue was the pleasing hue
    Of the Tickletoeteaser's claws.
And we sat on the edge of a sandy ledge
    And shot at the whistling bee;
And the Binnacle-bats wore waterproof hats
    As they danced in the sounding sea.

On a rubagub bark, from dawn to dark,
    We fed, till we all had grown
Uncommonly shrunk,—when a Chinese junk
    Came by from the torribly zone.
She was stubby and square, but we didn't much care,
    And we cheerily put to sea;
And we left the crew of the junk to chew
    The bark of the rubagub tree.

—Charles Edward Carryl

There was a young farmer of Leeds,
Who swallowed six packets of seeds.
　　It soon came to pass
　　He was covered with grass,
And he couldn't sit down for the weeds.

—*Anonymous*

Going Too Far

A woman who lived in Holland, of old,
Polished her brass till it shone like gold.
She washed her pig after all his meals
In spite of his energetic squeals.
She scrubbed her doorstep into the ground,
And the children's faces, pink and round,
She washed so hard that in several cases
She polished their features off their faces—
Which gave them an odd appearance, though
She thought they were really neater so!

Then her passion for cleaning quickly grew,
And she scrubbed and polished the village through,
Until, to the rage of all the people,
She cleaned the weather-vane off the steeple.
As she looked at the sky one summer's night
She thought that the stars shone out less bright;
And she said with a sigh, "If I were there,
I'd rub them up till the world should stare."

That night a storm began to brew,
And a wind from the ocean blew and blew
Till, when she came to her door next day
It whisked her up, and blew her away—
Up and up in the air so high
That she vanished, at last, in the stormy sky.
Since then it's said that each twinkling star
And the big white moon, shine brighter far.
But the neighbors shake their heads in fear
She may rub so hard they will disappear!

—Mildred Howells

A flea and a fly in a flue
Were imprisoned, so what could they do?
      Said the fly, "Let us flee,"
      Said the flea, "Let us fly,"
So they flew through a flaw in the flue.

—*Anonymous*

The Fastidious Serpent

There was a snake that dwelt in Skye,
    Over the misty sea, oh;
He lived upon nothing but gooseberry pie
    For breakfast, dinner and tea, oh.

Now gooseberry pie—as is very well known,—
    Over the misty sea, oh,
Is not to be found under every stone,
    Nor yet upon every tree, oh.

And being so ill to please with his meat,
    Over the misty sea, oh;
The snake had sometimes nothing to eat,
    And an angry snake was he, oh.

Then he'd flick his tongue and his head he'd shake,
    Over the misty sea, oh,
Crying, "Gooseberry pie! For goodness' sake,
    Some gooseberry pie for me, oh."

And if gooseberry pie was not to be had,
    Over the misty sea, oh,
He'd twine and twist like an eel gone mad,
    Or a worm just stung by a bee, oh.

But though he might shout and wriggle about,
    Over the misty sea, oh,
The snake had often to go without
    His breakfast, dinner and tea, oh.

—*Henry Johnstone*

The Common Cormorant

The common cormorant or shag
Lays eggs inside a paper bag.
The reason you will see no doubt
It is to keep the lightning out.
But what these unobservant birds
Have never noticed is that herds
Of wandering bears may come with buns
And steal the bags to hold the crumbs.

—*Anonymous*

The Crocodile

How doth the little crocodile
    Improve his shining tail,
And pour the waters of the Nile
    On every golden scale!

How cheerfully he seems to grin,
    How neatly spreads his claws,
And welcomes little fishes in
    With gently smiling jaws!

—*Lewis Carroll*

The Ostrich Is a Silly Bird

The ostrich is a silly bird,
　　With scarcely any mind.
He often runs so very fast,
　　He leaves himself behind.

And when he gets there, has to stand
　　And hang about till night,
Without a blessed thing to do
　　Until he comes in sight.

—*Mary E. Wilkins Freeman*

The Quangle Wangle's Hat

On the top of the Crumpetty Tree
    The Quangle Wangle sat,
But his face you could not see,
    On account of his Beaver Hat.
For his Hat was a hundred and two feet wide,
With ribbons and bibbons on every side,
And bells, and buttons, and loops, and lace,
So that nobody ever could see the face
    Of the Quangle Wangle Quee.

The Quangle Wangle said
    To himself on the Crumpetty Tree,
"Jam, and jelly, and bread
    Are the best of food for me!
But the longer I live on this Crumpetty Tree
The plainer than ever it seems to me
That very few people come this way
And that life on the whole is far from gay!"
    Said the Quangle Wangle Quee.

But there came to the Crumpetty Tree
    Mr. and Mrs. Canary;
And they said, "Did you ever see
    Any spot so charmingly airy?
May we build a nest on your lovely Hat?
Mr. Quangle Wangle, grant us that!
Oh, please let us come and build a nest,
Of whatever material suits you best,
    Mr. Quangle Wangle Quee!"

And besides, to the Crumpetty Tree
    Came the Stork, the Duck, and the Owl;
The Snail and the Bumble Bee,
    The Frog and the Fimble Fowl
(The Fimble Fowl, with a corkscrew leg);
And all of them said, "We humbly beg
We may build our homes on your lovely Hat—
Mr. Quangle Wangle, grant us that!
    Mr. Quangle Wangle Quee!"

And the Golden Grouse came there,
   And the Pobble who has no toes,
And the small Olympian Bear,
   And the Dong with a luminous nose.
And the Blue Baboon who played the flute,
And the Orient Calf from the Land of Tute,
And the Attery Squash, and the Bisky Bat—
All came and built on the lovely Hat
   Of the Quangle Wangle Quee!

And the Quangle Wangle said
    To himself on the Crumpetty Tree,
"When all these creatures move
    What a wonderful noise there'll be!"
And at night by the light of the Mulberry Moon
They danced to the Flute of the Blue Baboon,
On the broad green leaves of the Crumpetty Tree,
And all were as happy as happy could be,
    With the Quangle Wangle Quee.

—Edward Lear